S0-CJQ-550

Ei   R514984
Sin   8.95
Singerman
Stephen's bag

DATE DUE		
DE 20'90	AUG 0 5 1994	
JAN 1 8 1991	SEP 0 9 1994	
JUN 2 2 1991		
AUG 1 5 1991	FEB 0 3 1995	
DEC 0 5 1991		
FEB 1 1 1992	FEB 2 3 1995	
AUG 0 7 1992	MAR 3 1 1995	
JUL 0 6 1993		
OCT 0 1 1993		
MAR 2 6 1994		

DE

GREAT RIVER REGIONAL LIBRARY

St. Cloud, Minnesota 56301

STEPHEN'S BAG

Written By Ellen Singerman
Illustrated By Art Kirchhoff

R 514984

146 7224

Milliken Publishing Company, St. Louis, Missouri

To my mother, who instilled in me a love for books.

E.S.

© 1987 by Milliken Publishing Company

All rights reserved. No part of this book may be used or reproduced in any manner whatsoever without written permission. Printed in the United States of America.

Series Editors: Patricia and Fredrick McKissack
Cover Design by Graphcom, Inc., St. Louis, Missouri
Logo Design by Justmann Associates, St. Louis, Missouri

Library of Congress Catalog Card Number: 87-61642
ISBN 0-88335-749-6 / ISBN 0-88335-729-1 (lib. bdg.)

Stephen had a special bag.
It was a sack full of fun and surprise.

1

From morning until night,
Stephen took his bag wherever he went.

He brought it here, then there, then back again.

In Stephen's bag, there was always
a big, blue marble,
a penny,
and a bakery number, 36.

There was a picture of his dog, Sam,
a small, white stone,

4

and a pine cone.
(The pine cone made the bag smell good.)

5

In Stephen's bag, there were bread crusts.
There were also raisins — always raisins —
sometimes four,
sometimes more.

In Stephen's bag, there was a ball of red yarn and a mitten full of watermelon seeds.

7

There was a sailor's cap,
a whistle,
a seashell,
and a handful of sand.

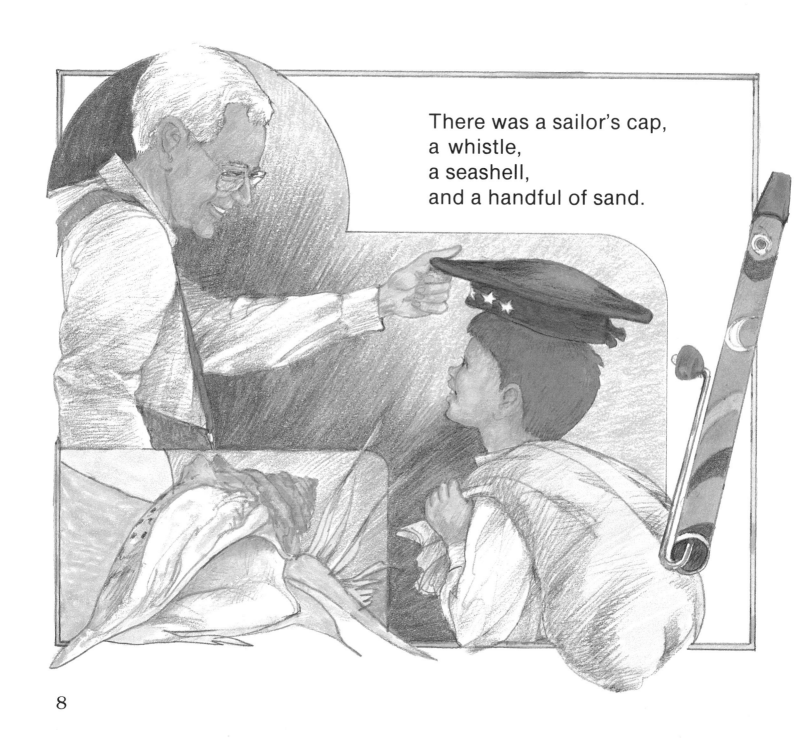

In Stephen's bag, there was a butterfly
he had caught in the forest.
There was also a crow's feather
and three shiny buttons:
one orange, one blue,
and a bright green one too.
Stephen added a tiny toad
to the treasures in his bag.

9

The toad in the bag
went home with Stephen

and jumped in a wet ball of noodles.

Then Stephen grabbed the toad
and ran out the door,

down the steps,

over the fence,

and into the field.

Stephen fell head over heels.

14

"KERPLOP!" went the bag in the mud.

Out slipped a barn key,
a bell,
and the queen of hearts.

16

But soon they were back in the sack.

18

Stephen found an old tin can
out behind the schoolhouse.
He kept it inside the bag.

In the old tin can,
Stephen kept pieces of the field
that he chewed on every day
and leftover noodles that looked like
worms to Stephen.

In Stephen's bag, there were always
very special things:
a magic stick,

a birthday card from his great-aunt Minnie,
a book he wanted to read one day,
and a dandelion too.

Stephen traded a fishing hook
for a diamond rock
Kelly McGarvey had found in the stream.

(Stephen always thought he had gotten the best deal.)

Down in the bottom of the sack,
under Gramps' pocket watch,
was Stephen's baby tooth —
the one the tooth fairy forgot to take.

27

Stephen's bag —
every day something new,
every day new treasures.

29

Vocabulary

a	card	gotten	marble	rusty	things
added	caught	grabbed	Minnie	sack	thought
again	chewed	Gramps	mitten	sailor	three
also	cone	great-aunt	more	Sam	tin
always	crow	green	morning	sand	tiny
an	crusts	had	mud	schoolhouse	to
and	dandelion	handful	new	seashell	toad
baby	day	he	night	seeds	too
back	deal	head	noodles	shiny	took
bag	diamond	hearts	number	slipped	tooth
bakery	dog	heels	of	small	traded
ball	door	here	old	smell	treasures
barn	down	his	on	something	under
behind	every	home	one	sometimes	until
bell	fairy	hook	orange	soon	very
best	feather	in	out	special	wanted
big	fell	inside	over	Stephen	was
birthday	fence	into	penny	steps	watch
blue	field	it	picture	stick	watermelon
book	fishing	jumped	pieces	stone	went
bottom	for	Kelly McGarvey	pine	stream	were
bread	forest	kept	pocket	surprise	wet
bright	forgot	key	queen	take	wherever
brought	found	leftover	raisins	that	whistle
but	four	like	ran	the	white
butterfly	from	looked	read	then	with
buttons	full	made	red	there	worms
can	fun	magic	rock	they	yarn
cap	good				